S0-BCJ-434

Don Gillmor   Pierre Pratt

The Boy Who Ate the World

(and the girl who saved it)

North Winds Press
An Imprint of Scholastic Canada Ltd.

The illustrations in this book were created in
Acrylic paints on Schut Acryl 360 gr. paper.

Display type was set in Hotsy Totsy.
The text type was set in
ITC Usherwood LT Medium.

Library and Archives Canada Cataloguing in Publication

Gillmor, Don
The boy who ate the world : and the girl who saved it / Don Gillmor ; Pierre Pratt, illustrator.
ISBN 978-0-439-94738-1
1. Picture books for children. I. Pratt, Pierre II. Title.

PS8563.I59B69 2008   jC813'.54   C2008-900829-4

ISBN-10 0-439-94738-3

Text copyright © 2008 by Don Gillmor
Illustrations copyright © 2008 by Pierre Pratt
All rights reserved.

No part of this publication may be reproduced or stored in a retrieval system,
or transmitted in any form or by any means, electronic, mechanical,
recording, or otherwise, without written permission of the publisher,
North Winds Press, an imprint of Scholastic Canada Ltd.,
604 King Street West, Toronto, Ontario M5V 1E1, Canada.
In the case of photocopying or other reprographic copying, a licence
must be obtained from Access Copyright (Canadian Copyright Licensing Agency),
1 Yonge Street, Suite 800, Toronto, Ontario M5E 1E5 (1-800-893-5777).

6 5 4 3 2 1   Printed in Singapore   08 09 10 11 12 13

NIAGARA FALLS PUBLIC LIBRARY

For M.E.
— *D.G.*

For Constança.
— *P.P.*

Herman Oof was huge.

This was no surprise, since his father was a giant. Mr. Oof's head was bigger than a pumpkin and his hands were like tennis rackets. He was so big that he drove three cars. The only thing bigger than Mr. Oof was Mrs. Oof, who towered over her husband like an oak tree.

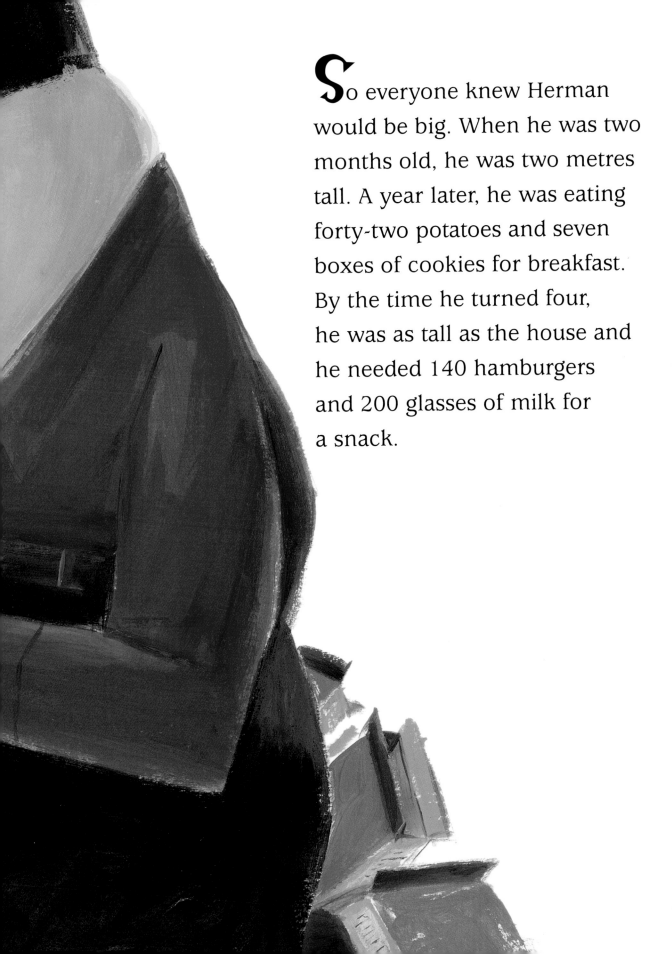

So everyone knew Herman would be big. When he was two months old, he was two metres tall. A year later, he was eating forty-two potatoes and seven boxes of cookies for breakfast. By the time he turned four, he was as tall as the house and he needed 140 hamburgers and 200 glasses of milk for a snack.

Scientists examined Herman and said, "If this keeps up, soon there won't be anything left to eat in the whole world."

6

"Don't be silly," Mr. Oof said. "The world's a big place. There's always something left."

On Herman's seventh birthday there was no cake, because he had eaten everything in his town. The Oofs moved to the biggest city they could find.

"Look at all the restaurants," Mrs. Oof said, as they drove along the streets in their giant truck, Herman sitting in the back like a mountain. "This is perfect."

But it only took six months to eat everything in the big city. All the restaurants and supermarkets closed, and the people moved away. Herman was lonely. He was too tall to talk to anyone.

He stared up at the sky and imagined that he was the moon

and the stars were all his friends. And he was hungry. Very hungry.

He ate a building. It wasn't bad. It tasted sort of like chicken. He tried another. Soon he had eaten the whole city.

It wasn't long before he had eaten the whole country. Which made him very thirsty. He drank the Atlantic Ocean, but it was salty and only made him thirstier. He rolled Greenland up like a burrito and ate it with raspberry jam.

He tried Africa with a bit of
peanut butter and it was pretty good,
although it stuck to the roof of his mouth. There weren't
many lakes left to drink, but he found a nice one in Russia.
After he finished the lake he fell asleep, his huge body
covering the country, his feet dangling
into the sea.

While he was sleeping, a small girl named Sarah climbed up on him and shouted in his ear. "Wake up, you big nincompoop!" she yelled.

Herman opened his eyes. "Who said that?"

"I did." Sarah swung around so she was perched on his nose.

"You've practically eaten the whole world," she said. "I hope you're happy."

Herman thought for a minute. "No," he said. "I'm not happy." He started munching on the coastline, without really thinking. The earth wasn't even round any more. It was shaped like a banana. There wasn't much left, and it was going fast.

"My name's Herman," Herman said, as he swallowed Australia.

"I'm Sarah," Sarah said. "You ate my dog."

"I ate everyone's dog," Herman said sadly. "I couldn't stop myself. I was just so hungry."

All that was left of the world now were the islands of Japan, which Herman popped into his mouth like peanuts.

"Well, that's just great," Sarah said, as they disappeared.

Herman was now the same shape as the earth, more or less. A huge, round thing with tiny legs and arms and a big moon face. Inside him, billions of people were wondering why it was so dark.

Herman and Sarah floated through space, revolving around the sun.

"I'm stuffed," Herman said. "I couldn't eat another bite."

"Really?" Sarah asked.

"I'd burst," Herman said. "Maybe I shouldn't have eaten China."

"You'd burst?" Sarah said.

"Absolutely."

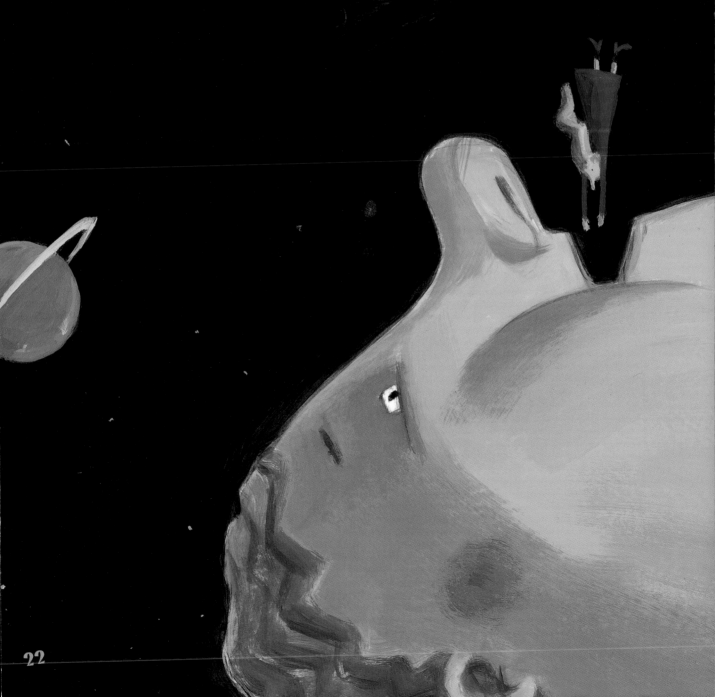

Sarah looked at Herman, at his giant, unhappy moon face. Then she jumped into his open mouth.

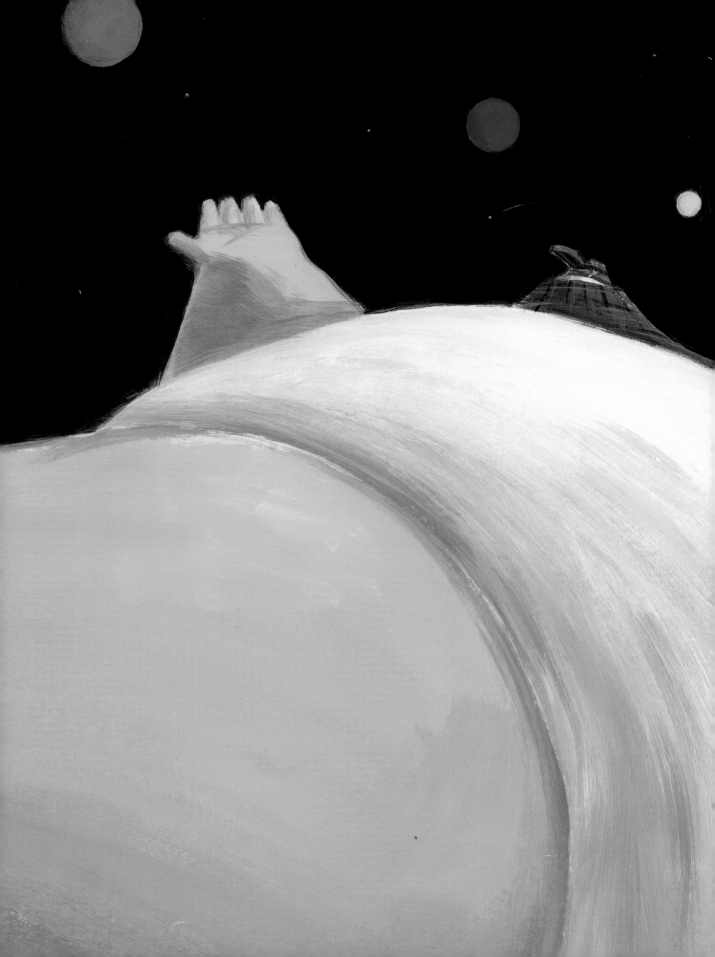

"**Noooooooo**," Herman wailed. Then he started to rumble. He started to quake. There was a giant whooshing sound, and Herman was suddenly gone.

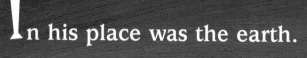n his place was the earth.

Some of the cities had teeth marks on them, and Africa was farther west than it had been before. The island of Ignatz had disappeared, and no one ever found the Burping Ocean. But there was the world.

Sarah called her dog. "Here, Stormy. Here, boy."
And Stormy came running.

They sat together on a hill and watched the
moon come out, which looked like Herman's face.
It was smiling.

"Well," Sarah said, "That was a close one."

AUG 1 5 2009